A Dublin Fairytale

Nicola Colton

THE O'BRIEN PRESS
DUBLIN

For my parents and Gavin.

NICOLA COLTON is an Irish illustrator;

A Dublin Fairytale is her first book.

Once upon a time, there was a little girl called Fiona who lived in Dublin with her mam.

'Granny is sick,' said Mam. 'She needs her special witches' brew to make her feel better. Will you go to the witches' market on Moore Street and buy the things she needs to make it? Then you can take them to Granny's house.'

'Take this map and follow the path I've drawn on it,' Mam said, 'Don't get delayed along the way. If anyone tries to talk to you, just tell them that you're in a hurry.'

Fiona put on her favourite red raincoat and set off through the trees of St Stephen's Green forest.

Then suddenly ...

Two of the trees weren't trees at all, but the legs of a giant!
Fiona was very afraid, but said in her bravest voice,
'I can't stop, I'm in a hurry!'

The giant looked at her sadly
and pointed to his foot.

'I am sorry if I startled you,
but I seem to be caught in a
thorn bush.'

'Well … maybe I can stop for a
minute,' Fiona said, as she
freed his foot.

'Oh, thank you!' said the giant ...

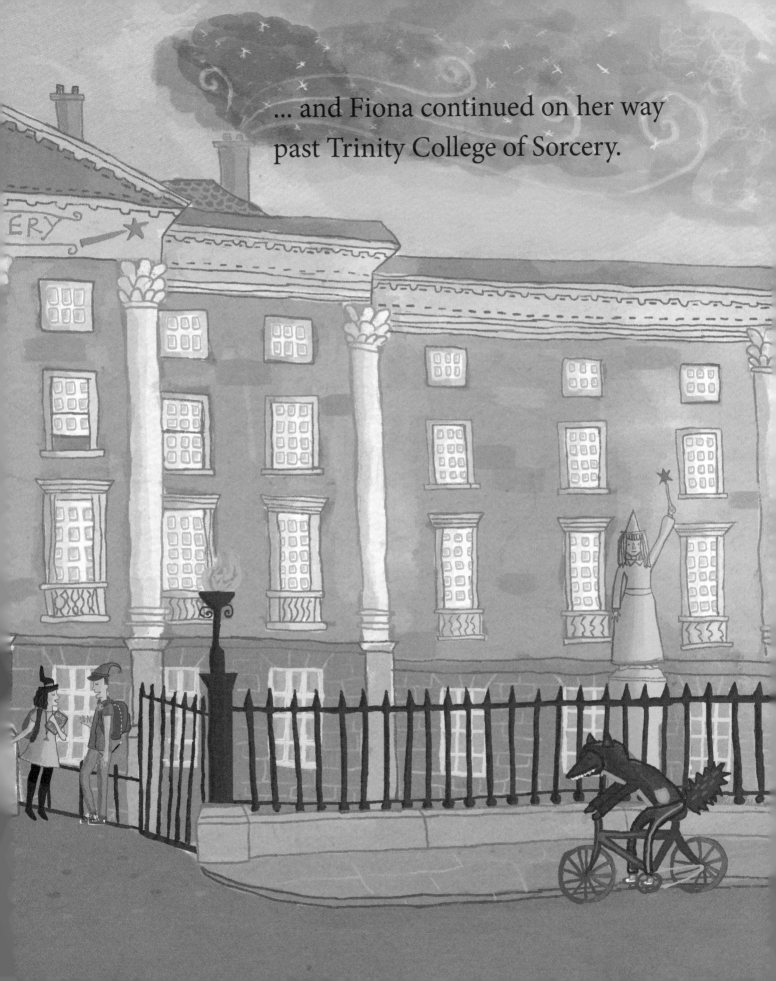

... and Fiona continued on her way past Trinity College of Sorcery.

She had just crossed the Ha'penny
Bridge, when suddenly ...

GGGGGrrrr!

Ha'penny Bridge

Fiona was very afraid, but said in her bravest voice, 'I can't stop, Mr Troll, I'm in a hurry!'

'I am sorry if I startled you, but I was just clearing my throat. It's very sore.'

'Well … maybe I can stop for a minute,' Fiona said and handed him a cough drop from her pocket.

'Oh, thank you!' said the troll, 'that feels much better.'

... and Fiona continued on her way.

She had just reached the Spire,
when suddenly …

Fiona was very afraid, but said in
her bravest voice,
'I can't stop, I'm in a hurry!'

'I am sorry if I startled you,' said the dragon, 'but there's a pigeon beside you and I am terribly frightened of them.'

'Well ... maybe I can stop for a minute,' Fiona said and chased the pigeon away.

'Oh, thank you!' said the dragon and Fiona continued on her way.

Fiona reached the market and was **amazed** at all the things for sale.

She bought everything she needed, but then suddenly–

Luckily, Fiona's new friends came to the rescue ...

'I'm sorry! I'm sorry!' the Wolf said. 'I just wanted some of your nice-smelling cake!'
'Well, you could have asked!' Fiona said. 'Come with me to Granny's and you can all have a slice.'

Granny was delighted to see Fiona and welcomed her new friends.

She made a pot of witches' brew for everyone –
and they **all** had a slice of cake.

First published 2015 by
The O'Brien Press Ltd,
12 Terenure Road East, Rathgar,
Dublin 6, D06 HD27, Ireland.
Tel: +353 1 4923333; Fax: +353 1 4922777
E-mail: books@obrien.ie
Website: www.obrien.ie
Reprinted 2015, 2016, 2017.
The O'Brien Press is a member of Publishing Ireland.

ISBN: 978-1-84717-774-2

8 7 6 5 4
20 19 18 17

Printed and bound in Poland by Białostockie Zakłady Graficzne S.A.
The paper in this book is produced using pulp from managed forests.

Published in
DUBLIN
UNESCO
City of Literature